Do You Love Me?
Copyright © 2009 by Joost Elffers and Curious Pictures
Manufactured in China.  All rights reserved. No part of this book may be used or
reproduced in any manner whatsoever without written permission except in the case
of brief quotations embodied in critical articles and reviews. For information address
HarperCollins Children's Books, a division of HarperCollins Publishers,
1350 Avenue of the Americas, New York, NY 10019.
www.harpercollinschildrens.com
Library of Congress Cataloging-in-Publication Data is available.
ISBN 978-0-06-166799-2 (trade bdg.) — ISBN 978-0-06-166800-5 (lib. bdg.)
3 4 5 6 7 8 9 10    ❖  First Edition

# do you love me?

joost elffers
+ curious pictures

the bowen press
*an imprint of* harpercollins*publishers*

do you love me?

always, dear.

do you need me?

ever near.

would you leave me?

never ever.

do you want me?

only forever.

can we nestle?

tender and slow.

am I special?

more than you know.

hug me,
hold me.

snug and tight.

snuzzle
closer.

kiss good night.